Lights Out, Night's Out

by

William Boniface

illustrated by

Milena Kirkova

Lights Out, Night's Out text copyright © 2009 by William Boniface.
Illustrations copyright © 2009 by Accord Publishing, a division of Andrews
McMeel Publishing, LLC. All rights reserved. Printed in China. No part of this
book may be used or reproduced in any manner whatsoever without written
permission except in the case of reprints in the context of reviews. For information,
write Accord Publishing, 1404 Larimer Street, Suite 200, Denver, CO 80202.

11 12 13 14 15 16 TEN 10 9 8 7 6 5 4 3 2 1

ISBN-13: 978-1-4494-0236-5
Library of Congress Control Number: 2010937865

www.accordpublishing.com

ACCORD PUBLISHING
a division of Andrews McMeel Publishing, LLC
Denver, Colorado

Nighttime's here,
Let's stretch and yawn.
You'll sleep all night,
Until the dawn.

But while you dream
'Til morning breaks,
Outside your door
A world awakes.

Roly-poly,
Prickly pear.
Who's that creature
Hiding there?

All rolled up.
A spiky ball.
Hedgehog hides
From one and all.

The cricket is
A crafty critter.
When the sun sets
Watch him skitter.

Here he jumps
And there he hops.
While it's dark
He never stops.

The moon's alone
Up in the sky.
The wolf can't help
But wonder why.

Hear him howl,
Head held high.
Hear his longing,
Lonely cry.

What does night mean
When you're blind?
Since dark is dark,
Bats hardly mind.

Watch them dodging,
Diving, dashing,
All the while,
Never crashing.

From the bushes,
Black eyes peek,
Dart about
And off they sneak.

Raccoon robbers
Shun the light,
Gather dusk
And steal the night.

Fireflies
Light up the night,
Making quite a
Shocking sight.

But buzzing songs
Are left unsung,
Silenced by
A sticky tongue!

The spider spins
Her silky web,
As evening breezes
Flow and ebb.

She flits along
That silken track,
Just waiting for
A midnight snack!

Soft paws press
Upon the ground,
Making hardly
Any sound.

A sudden halt.
Her tail bounces.
Eyes glow bright.
Jaguar pounces!

Who's that rising
From the swamp,
Getting ready
For a romp?

Hippos wake up
From their snooze,
Clomping, stomping
In the ooze.

Even creatures
Close to home
Like to use
The dark to roam.

Though they clatter
Through the night,
They're fast asleep
By morning's light.

Shining Light on Nocturnal Creatures

Spider web silk is about as strong as nylon, but stretches much farther.

Want to know how warm it is? Count **cricket** chirps for 15 seconds. Adding 40 to the total will tell you the air temperature in Fahrenheit.

Fireflies flash signals in different patterns as a way of talking to each other.

If there's water close by, a **raccoon** will douse its food, turning it over in the water and removing unwanted parts. They're not really washing it, just checking it out with their paws.

Wolves howl alone if they're lost or lonely, and together if they're celebrating. A wolf's howl can be heard as far as 10 miles (16 km) away.

Frogs use their sticky tongues to grab bugs as they fly by. It takes less than a second for the tongue to shoot out, grab a bug, and reel it in.

If a **hedgehog** is scared, it will protect itself by rolling into a tight ball with all of its spines sticking straight out.

Bats don't see very well, but have great hearing. They find their way by making noises and listening for the echoes.

A **hamster** can run as far as 5 miles (8 km) on its wheel in a single night.

Jaguars like to live alone, and scrape trees to mark their territories. The markings warn other animals to stay away.

Owls have feathers on their wings with special edges that help them to fly without making any noise. These feathers help them to be better hunters.

Hippos make their own sunscreen. It coats their skin so the parts of them that are above water don't get sunburned.